SIMON & SCHUSTER BOOKS FOR YOUNG READERS
An imprint of Simon & Schuster • Children's Publishing Division
• 1230 Avenue of the Americas, • New York, New York 10020
• Copyright © 2017 by Emily Gravett • Originally published
in Great Britain in 2017 by Macmillan Children's Books •
First US edition 2018 • All rights reserved, including the
right of reproduction in whole or in part in any form. •
SIMON & SCHUSTER BOOKS FOR YOUNG READ-
ERS is a trademark of Simon & Schuster, Inc. • For
information about special discounts for bulk purchases,
please contact Simon & Schuster Special Sales at
1-866-506-1949 or business@simonandschuster.com.
• The Simon & Schuster Speakers Bureau can bring
authors to your live event. For more information
or to book an event, contact the Simon & Schuster Speakers Bureau at 1-866-248-3049 or visit
our website at www.simonspeakers.com. • The
text for this book was set in Goudy Old Style
Std. • The illustrations for this
book were rendered in pencil,
watercolor, and acrylic ink.
• Manufactured in China •
1217 SUK • CIP data for
this book is available from the Library of Congress. • ISBN
978-1-5344-0917-0 • ISBN 978-1-5344-0958-3 (eBook)

2 4 6 8 10 9 7 5 3 1

SIMONANDSCHUSTER.COM/KIDS

For Sonny

Emily Gravett

OLD HAT

Simon & Schuster Books for Young Readers

New York   London   Toronto   Sydney   New Delhi

Harbet had a hat.

His Nana had knitted it for him when he was little.

It was warm and cozy, and it kept his ears toasty.

It was an . . .

OLD
HAT!

So Harbet got a new hat.

The latest hat!

It was fashionable, fresh, and fun.

It was low in fat,
high in fiber, and
could provide 80%
of his daily vitamins.

It was the latest,
most up-to-datest
hat there was.

Until . . .

It wasn't.

HA HA HA

So Harbet got a *new* new hat.

This hat really was the latest thing.
It came with a state-of-the-art flashing light
and was highly visible to oncoming traffic.

But when Harbet put on his hat and went outside . . .

Harbet was determined to have the latest hat.
He bought *Top Hat* magazine,

and was the first in line at the hat shop
on Hat Unveiling Day.

But whatever Harbet tried . . .

OLD HAT! OLD

HAT! OLD HAT!

Harbet had had enough.

So one day he did something no one had ever done before. . . .

Harbet took off his hat.

My best Old Hat
SAVE FOR WINTER

FRAGILE

FEB   2018